Hello,

This little star is Me and this beautiful unicorn is Bibi. We are very happy about you joining us for our journey to the Big Adventure. I have arrived here to Earth a long time ago, and have met one of the last unicorns alive on this planet and now we are best friends. We wander around the world, we get to know new animals, countries, we learn new things... so join us to experience awesome adventures.

Let's settle here

Welcome to our first adventure. Me and Bibi have decided to go to the toy garden to build our House. A long way has led to the garden, but we did it. It is beautiful in here, there are flowers, trees and, of course, toys everywhere. Toys are everywhere we look, it is amazing! Toys are in the water, bushes, trees as if they fell down from the sky. We decided to look around and look for some toy house for us. We have been looking for a long time, not even hoping to find it. Finally, probably because we didn't give up, we found it. It was goergous, colorful and big, and housed in a cozy glade near a small lake with a waterfall. It was exactly for us and we knew right away that we would move in here and want to stay. We started furnishing our cozy house. We started to slowly collect the toys so they would be close to our house. And then it happened – our neighbors visited us. It was unexpected, but they were a nice group of Dwarves. We became friends and showed them our new house. The Dwarves were very talkative and told us about a place where they look for gold. Me and Bibi found it strange why they need gold when they live in a land full of toys. The Dwarves took us on an adventurous expedition to the mine to show us how hard they have to work to get gold. The mine was huge. Me and Bibi tried the quarrying and to tell the truth, it was hard work. But we still didn't understand why they have to work so hard so we asked them and they explained it to us. So listen, gold is important to Botchers – the most experienced masters of all. The Dwarves took us to their workrooms. It took us a while to get there. As we were approaching the workrooms we saw piles and piles of broken toys and then we realized. The Botchers are master repairmens who have their workrooms inside the trees and repair broken toys. There is a lot of broken toys because children don't know how to play with the toys. That's why the Dwarves and Botchers have to work hard so they can manage to repair all the toys. Me and Bibi thanked the Dwarves and Botchers and went home to prepare for another adventure. And you, children, play with your toys carefully so that the Dwarves and Botchers don't have to work hard all day and night.

Let's have a look at flying stars

As it is a tradition to look at the flying stars every year, so this year me and Bibi went to look at at the stars flying past our beautiful Earth. „It's here, it's here!" Bibi was shouting from the outside, „Come quickly!" And then it started. We watched all the stars flying from one side to the other. It was a huge amount of them. I decided to tell Bibi about my flight around the Earth. „Bibi come here. Let me tell you a story." It was a beautiful warm day and me and my friends stars were flying through the universe. We were flying together for years, saw a lot of planets and visited different corners of the universe. I will tell you about some of them later. So, we were flying until we arrived in a galaxy called Milky Way. It was incredibly colorful and as we were flying among different planets I noticed this blue Earth full of life. I decided I wanted to visit and if I like it in here, I'm gonna explore the whole planet. And I have been here for 7 years now. And I am not planning on leaving, because I have not discovered even half of this beauty. „Wow, so that is how you came to this Earth!" Bibi said. „Hey Bibi, let's wave at them. I am sure they still remember me. Yes, yes, let's try this... look! They waved back! And you know what? Wish for something." Here on Earth, it's a tradition to wish for something everytime my friends stars fly past the Earth. And the stars, from all their generosity and kindness, try very hard to fulfill even the most secret wishes everytime. I know this because I used to be one of them.

Visiting a Mysterious Land

....and here is another adventure. The Botchers have told us about a Mysterious Land where ice cream flows in all rivers, the trees have turned into lollipops and land is covered with candy. But that's not all. There are chocolate animals everywhere you look. So me and Bibi decided to fly there. It took a lot of time. We flew for hours, maybe even days. We asked everyone we'd met to navigate us and then it happened. We arrived on beautiful island, but it looked nothing like the land described by our friends Botchers. We were very tired from our journey so we decided to stay overnight. We made ourselves comfortable places to sleep in and fell asleep. After we woke up in the morning, we decided to explore the island. We were searching and looking but without any success. When we had no more hope, we bumped into a cave. There was a text above the entrance that we tried to solve and managed to read it. It said: welcome to the Mysterious Land. Me and Bibi got very excited about finding the place. We were a bit scared, but decided to step inside anyways. It was dark but after a while we stepped outside into a light. „Yaay!" Bibi said and we started to explore the new place. It was exactly like our friends Botchers described it, even better. Bibi ran to the river and ate the ice cream. I ran to the first tree I saw and licked it all. It was amazing. A lot of chocolate animals came to us and offered us to take a bite of them. They tasted great. After a while, me and Bibi were overfilled with all the sweets so we decided to relax and continue in our feast later. We went to explore this mysterious land and the chocolate animals accompanied us until they led us to a huge gingerbread castle. We stepped in front of the front door and knocked. The door opened and Marshmellows welcomed us. They invited us to greet Marshmellow King. Marshmellow King greeted us and offered us all different types of sweets. There were 7 kinds of ice cream on the table, chocolate soup, licorice cutlets, candy, gums, lollipops and juice for drinking. This all was for us. Marshmellow King offered us a sightseeing of the castle after we finished eating... everything was beautiful and majestic. But we thought something was missing there and we were right. Everyone was missing a smile. King admitted that Caries-eaters have been making troubles in the kingdom for a while. They would steal a smile from everyone's face in the kingdom. Me and Bibi decided to help worried King and wanted to find a solution. They sent us to visit Owl Polymath that lived in Lollipop Forest. We were travelling for 4 days and 4 nights until we found it. Owl told us one and only secret way that would stop the Caries-eaters and make Marshmellows and you smile. I'm sure you know what I'm talking about, so go wash your teeth so Marshmellows can smile again! „Thank you!" King Marshmellow said and walked us outside the dark cave into the beautiful island. „What's next?" Bibi asked me. „To another adventure, of course!" I answered with a smile on my face.

Zoo

.....it's here. Me and Bibi decided to visit the local zoo to see local animals and maybe even feed them if they let us, of course. The entrance gate was huge as the highest skyscraper. We stepped towards it and bought tickets by a window. „Here we are!" Bibi said all excited. We ran to the first outlet full of mighty Mouselephants immediately. Do you not know this kind? Oh, I must have forgotten to tell you that we are not going to a regular zoo. We're going to a Magic Zoo, where animals of all kinds of fantasy exist. So let's get back to our Mouselephants. A Mouselephant is a magic animal that is as big as an elephant is, but it looks like a mouse. What is interesting about them is that everytime they sneeze from both of their trunks, they sneeze out a pink dust that smells amazingly. Me and Bibi waited and waited until one of those mighty Mouselephants would sneeze. „Aaa look Bibi! It looks like it's happening." „Achooo."the biggest Mouselephant sneezed. That was a lot of dust. There was a pink cloud of scented dust everywhere around us. It was great but once we saw it, it was enough and we walked to another outlet. Look! These are Waterbirds. They were amazing, how they flew around, then sunk under water and swam. Something unbelievable. If the name of these animals doen't really say anything to you, let me tell you something about them. They are these little creatures that look like fish, but each one of them has huge wings that work both for swimming and flying. Isn't that perfect? We were looking at them with Bibi for about 10 minutes because there were hundreds of them and they created beautiful patterns together in the sky and water as well. Soon, me and Bibi went to look at another kind of animals and it couldn't be nothing else than Crocopedes. That is an animal looking like a crocodile but has hundred legs. The table by the outlet said there are three of them. We only saw one but that was something. I had never seen that many legs. „And look how synchonized they are." Bibi said. „Yes, you're right." It was like the sound of drums, so loud and accurate. „I wouldn't want to get shoes on this one." Bibi laughed. „Me neither" I agreed and ordered to go to another outlet where a family of Monknails were waiting for us.

That is a strange kind, mixture of a monkey and a snail. Monknails are very slow. They have a big blue shell on their backs where they hide when they go to sleep in the evening. They are very cute when they move so slowly on the tree branches. And there's one last animal awaiting us before we go back home. We left the best for the last so let's have a look together. We were approaching the last outlet when we heard it. It was mighty Kinger. It's something amazing. So, this Kinger is as big as a cat is, but has a colorful mane around its head that slightly shines. What's bes tis that Kinger is the best singer in the whole magic land. Kinger can do all the sounds of the world. So if we stay for a while, we can hear different kinds of birds, sound of the sea and river and there's a gossip that Kinger can do the sound of growing grass. „Wow, that is something!" Bibi shouted, „I'd want to hear that." .„Me too."I said, „But we don't have time. We have to get back home before it gets dark outside.". So then, friends, we have to hurry home and we will see you on another adventure. Bye!

Carousels

„ME!" Bibi woke me up in the early morning. „What is so important that you need to wake me up so early?" I asked. „Breakfast is important, of course!" Bibi said with a smile on her face. „Yes, that's right, Bibi."I agreed. „And you know what else ME? Carousels are arriving today to our forest, yaay! We're going to turn around, slide, play and have a lot of fun!" That's true, I said and ran out of bed to eat breakfast. Bibi prepared cereals with milk and orange juice just how I love it. After we finished our breakfast, we prepared so we could head out to see the carousels. We packed everything important and headed out. It was not far away but we wanted to stop by to see our friends and take them with us. It would be more fun with a group of friends. The first friend we visited was a forest fairy Flower. We were hoping she would go because she always has a lot of responsibilities. She is the one who has to take care of all the flowers so they look and smell beautifully. She flies all over meadows and forests to take care of all the pretty flowers. So we arrived, knocked on the wooden door but nobody answered. It was clear to us that she was flying from one flower to another so we went to visit fairy Tooth. We know that Tooth works mainly during nights, so we hope she would come and have fun with us. Even without knocking, she already opened the door and greeted us with smile and hugs. „Hello, my friends! What are you doing in here?" she asked. „Carousels!" Bibi answered. Tooth's eyes widened and we knew she would join us. She packed her stuff quickly, locked her house and we could go to the carousels. As we were walking, Tooth told us about her job, so listen to this. „Ah, kids, I love my job! I fly to children's bedrooms everyday where I arrive very quietly, I take a tooth from below the pillow where the child left it and, of course, I leave there something to make the child happy." .„Like what?" curious Bibi interrupted her. „Usually, it's money or sweets." Tooth continued. „And what do you do with all the teeth then?" Bibi asked. „I immediately take it to our headquarters and what we do there is a huge secret, but we can talk about it in the next book." Me and Bibi agreed and there it was. We could hear music and see lights. We were really close and it didn't take us long and we arrived to the carousels. It was great! Carousels were everywhere – big, small, turning, still and rocking. We could smell the cotton candy and had to buy some immediately. I got yellow, Bibi had white and Tooth bought herself beautiful pink one. After we finished eating we went to do some carousels. It took us almost whole day, we tried almost every carousel there and we agreed that the best one was the big one called Coachell. We were sitting in a cabin and were going up and down, turning to the front and then back all over again. It was so much fun! It was slowly starting to get dark so me and Tooth jumped on Bibi's back and she took us to Tooth's house (because unicorns can fly). „Friends, thank you for an amazing day!" Tooth said. „We thank you as well!" me and Bibi replied together. We said goodbye and went to our house in the toy garden. Right after we got back home, we changed our clothes and brushed our teeth. I read one more story to Bibi who opened her tired eyes afterwards and said: „Thank you and we wish you sweet dreams, our friends. We will see you on our next exciting adventure……"

Toys and North Pole

Hello, friends! Me and Bibi were thinking... have you ever thought about were all the toys are made? We decided to explore and find out. We asked all our friends and their answers were clear. Toys have to be made on the North Pole. Me and Bibi packed all of our warm clothes, gloves, hats, sweaters, even scarfs, and went on a long and cold journey to the North Pole. Journey was supposed to lead through four kingdoms, two seas and one desert. We prepared responsibly so nothing on our journey could surprise us. Everything went smoothly and we got to the borders of the North Pole. We were dressed properly and could wade through all the snow. It was much more harder than we'd thought it would be. Sometimes, snow was up to our necks and only our heads could be seen. We were wandering the whole day and suddenly – huge snow storm. We couldn't see anything so me and Bibi hugged each other and slowly went step by step together. But as soon as the storm came, it also disappeared. When we opened our eyes, we were standing in front of a cave. We stepped inside and decided to stay overnight. We settled in, unpacked our things and set up fire. While we were sitting by the fire, we heard a voice coming from depth of the cave. At first, something cracked, then it sounded as footsteps. As if something was approaching us, something big. It was louder and louder and coming closer to us. We had no idea what to do, we just stayed there as if we froze. After a few seconds, a giant came out of the darkness. It was brown and furry and had big eyes, hands and legs – it was huge. Me and Bibi were so scared we couldn't even say anything. Until the moment when the giant opened its mouth, showed its big teeth and said: „Hi, my name is Yetti."and smiled at us. „Phew." Bibi sighed and me as well. „Hi there, my name is Me and this is Bibi. Nice to meet you." Everything was fine, there was nothing to be afraid of. Yetti told us that it's been living there for hundreds of years and took us deeper into the cave to show us its Ice House. We told him we are on our way to the North Pole to discover Toy Kingdom where all the toys are made. Yetti offered to accompany us so we wouldn't get lost. Obviously, he knew where everything was. The next day, we headed out first thing in the morning, took a shorter way and arrived there at noon. Great, the North Pole! But there was nothing except for one red pole with a table on it saying "North Pole". We were a bit disappointed but we would never give up. Bibi noticed small letters at the bottom of the table saying: "Knock three times for the entrance.". „Knock, knock, knock." Bibi knocked on the table and, suddenly, earth below us started to shake. We started to move downwards into the grouns as if we were in an elevator. The elevator stopped and then we saw it. „Wooow!" Bibi screamed. We couldn't believe our own eyes. We were there – a big toy factory in front of us. There were millions of little green elfs running around who designed, made, moved, carried and even wrapped all the toys. We were so fascinated. Even Yetti didn't know what to say because he'd never been there before. It was amazing, we were out of our minds and suddenly a big yellow elf came up to us. „Hello, I am a master elf and I will show you around.". All kinds of toys were in there. We walked around and looked at all the elfs working, but we were mostly amazed by all the toys, balls, dolls, cars, wooden, plastic and metallic toys, toys controlled by command and toys pulled by a rope. At the end of the excursion, master elf allowed each of us to take one toy away as a reward for being nice. I took a stuffed unicorn, Bibi took a stuffed star and Yetti took s stuffed snowball. And what about you, friends? What toy would you choose? Unicorn or rather a star?

Let's go Swimming

It was nice warm summer day and me and Bibi wanted to go swimming with our friends, but something wasn't right. I looked at Bibi and she was all pale and I had a flu. Oh no! We must have gotten sick on the North Pole. Both me and Bibi were sick so we couldn't go swimming. „Miracle would need to happen so we could go swimming today." Bibi said. As it is said, you know your true friend during hard times – in our case, Tooth came. It was early in the morning and as soon as she saw us, she knew what it was. She ran outside into the garden and stocked up two full baskets. One was full of vegetables and the other full of fruit. We got medicine, now it was time for treatment. She got into the treatment, chopped, cooked, made some vegetable potions and effective soups. Me and Bibi were lying in bed, sweating and looking at her working. It was almost noon and Tooth serve dus the medicine. Without saying anything, we started eating. It was all fruits and vegetables and it tasted amazingly, yummy! After we finished eating I felt much better. When I looked over at Bibi, she looked totally healthy. „It is all thanks to the fruits and vegetables. " Tooth said. It's so full of vitamins, it drove away all the illness. And that's not everything – if you'll eat fruits and vegetables often, you won't get sick at all and you can run outside with friends the whole day, whether it's summer or winter. And now, hurry up to the swimming pool because we are already ten minutes late. „Yaay, let's go swimming!" Bibi screamed with excitement. We packed all the necessary stuff like swimsuit, inflatable wheels and were ready to swim. So then, friends, don't dorget to ear fruits and vegetables in order to run outside with your friends!

Let's go to the Universe

Here comes the day D. Me and Bibi had been preparing for this day for a long time so we'd be fit. Conditions for traveling into the universe are demanding, but we did it. Morning was peaceful, weather was pretty, only Bibi seemed a bit off. „What's wrong, Bibi?" I asked. „I'm a little bit scared." She answered. „Don't be. We can do this together." I calmed her down. „Okay then." She agreed and we started packing so we could head to the universe airport. „Do we have everything?" Bibi asked. „I don't think so. But if not, then it was not important!" I smiled. The airport wasn't far from our home, only two days of travel. The journey led through an old forest, through the Pink lake, then to the meadow of happy fairies, where we decided to sleepover. We built our tent and set up fire so we could bake our bread. As the fire was burning and it was getting darker, hundreds of fairies came to our tent. We didn't talk a lot because they have their own language we couldn't understand. But they were smiling at us the whole time and would sing and dance around the fire. It was nice. As we were sitting and enjoying the atmosphere that the fairies created, Bibi looked at me and pointed to the sky. It was clear and full of stars. „I know, Bibi. We're heading there. Can you see Great Bear?" I asked. „Yes, yes! And look, there's the small one." She said. „And this, Bibi, is Orion. And the brightest star in the sky is my friend Sirius." We were amazed by the beautiful sky and then went to sleep. The night passed by quickly and morning was nice even though we were a bit stiff. Sleeping in a tent on the ground is definitely not as comfortable as sleeping on mattress back home. We left in the early morning because we were supposed to arrive to the universe airport that day. Journey through the golden mountain where dwarves look for gold awaited us. We arrived to the airport around noon. Me and Bibi ate amazing lunch and got ready for the next flight to the universe. We dropped off our baggage that was moved to a spaceship. Me and Bibi were then moved to a special room where we got these funny uniforms and big round helmets. When we were ready, they took us to the spaceship board. When we got there, speakers said: „Welcome on board of the Galaxic. Settle down, buckle in and make yourselves comfortable. We're going to take off in five minutes." And it's here. Those five minutes passed by quickly and the voice from the speakers said: „Get ready in 5, 4, 3, 2, 1.... we're flying! First stop – Moon." It was so exciting! Flight was supposed to take couple of hours so me and Bibi decided we'd sleep. And you, my friends, go to sleep as well and we'll meet on another adventure in the universe. Bye!

In the Universe

„Dear passengers, we're landing on the Moon, soon." voice from the speakers announced. Me and Bibi got all excited. We couldn't sleep as much as we wanted to because of turbulences and then, we looked at all the beauties of the universe and our planet from from distance. It was very ineteresting and exciting journey and we wouldn't even imagine going into the universe. While we were landing I looked at Bibi and she looked totally calm, which was not my case since I was a bit off. But everything ended up just fine. „Welcome on the Moon! Put on your cosmo uniforms and gather by the main exit." Me and Bibi were already prepared so we could step on the Moon as the first ones. It was worth it, we were far ahead of everyone. They took a while to get ready but we didn't mind. The only thing we could think of was how the door open and we step outside. „Look! The door is finally opening, it's here!" Bibi screamed. Orange light turned on above the door and it was true – the door started opening. It was a few seconds and me and Bibi finally stepped on the Moon. „Woow!" Bibi was amazed. It's totally different. Walking on the Moon is more easy and comfortable. Firstly, we waited for everyone to gather outside the spaceship and create couples to walk in on the Moon. When everyone was ready, we could head to the Moon headquarters. The spaceship captain showed us everything around and answered all the questions while we were walking. Bibi asked him a question about this huge hole near us. „Mr Captain, what is that big hole and how was it created?" „That is a crater and the whole Moon is covered with it. It's created when a big meteorite falls down on the Moon." He answered. „Woow, this one must have been huge!" Bibi said with excitement.after a while we saw the Moon headquarters. It was at least ten times bigger than our spaceship. We were ready to go inside but before that, a huge fan had to blow off all the dust from us. After that, we stepped inside and saw all the strangers from a faraway universe. They were green, had three finger and were very small. Aliens. When we were taking off from the Earth, we were told we could meet them and it happened. They were really nice so we talked and they told us something about their planet while we told them about ours. It wasn't that different. They made hot chocolate for us and gave us some biscuits. They were great! Unfortunately, we had to leave so we said goodbye and went back to our spaceship. Soon, we were sitting in the spaceship ready to head back to our beautiful planet Earth. „Buckle in and have a pleasant journey on the way back!" speakers announced. Me and Bibi chuckled and decided to take a nap after this long tiring day. And you, our friends, how was you day? Thank you for being a part of our universe adventure and we're excited to meet you on our next adventure, bye!

Dino Saur

        It was warm sunny day and we had nothing to do. As we were relaxing, a dinosaur passed by our house. We couldn't believe our own eyes because we hadn't seen one before. Me and Bibi immediately packed everything essential and followed footsteps of the dinosaur in order to get into a DinoLand we heard of before but nobody could tell us where it is. It was super secret. We followed the footsteps until we could see the dinosaur in front of us again. It was quite slow but suddenly, it sped up as if it knew we were there. A few meter later it took a turn to the mirror waterfall. Something we didn't expect happened – it stepped inside the waterfall. We waited for a while, discussed it and decided to follow. We saw a light at the end of a tunnel when we stepped in and followed that light. When we reached the end, an amazing view on the whole DinoLand awaited us. There were at least thousand dinosaurs of different kinds – big ones with long necks called Brontosaurs, little ones with feathers that looked like chicken, flying ones, also the ones in the water. Basically, all the kinds of dinosaurs you know were there. „Welcome to the DinoLand!" the dinosaur we followed greeted us. „Hi! We're sorry we followed you, but we'd never seen any dinosaur before and we wanted to get to know you more." We said. „Yes, I understand. We don't come out of the DinoLand a lot. Only if it's really necessary." the dinosaur replied. „So, what made you to come out today?" Bibi asked. „I had a dentist appointment." he answered. „Well, that is very important." Bibi commented. „Exactly, you have to take proper care of your teeth. Brushing them every morning and evening, otherwise a bad caries will occur and thas is a lot of pain. But enough of the teeth, let me walk you around the DinoLand since you're already here. Oh, I almost forgot to introduce myself. That's obviously very polite. My name is Dino Saur. Friends call me Dino."Dino said. „My name is Me and this is Bibi. We're happy we could meet you." we introduced ourselves. „Let's go then!" Dino led us down to the valley to show us how dinosaurs live, what do their houses look like and to introduce us to others. First group was Brontosaurs who were so great they let us slide down their backs straight into the water. „Yaaay!" Bibi was all excited. Then, we visited

Pterodactyls who took us on a flight over the DinoLand. We flew over rivers, lakes and even a volcano full of hot lava. The last one was a family of T-rexes who invited us over to their home and showed us their babies. They were very restless and Bibi was running around with them. Walking from one group of dinosaurs to another took us the whole day but that's fine because it was amazing. In the end, we said goodbye to Dino and got back home. So, dear friends, we are excited for another adventure. Bye! Bye and see you in our next book....

THE END.......

Place for ART:

Try to draw how Me and Bibi are playng with Toys

Try to draw how Me and Bibi are sailing on the ocean

Place for ART

Try to draw how Me and Bibi lost in a desert

Try to draw how Me and Bibi are Diving (sea)

Try to draw a DinoSaur

Try to draw a SMILE

Try to draw a new animal from Magic Zoo

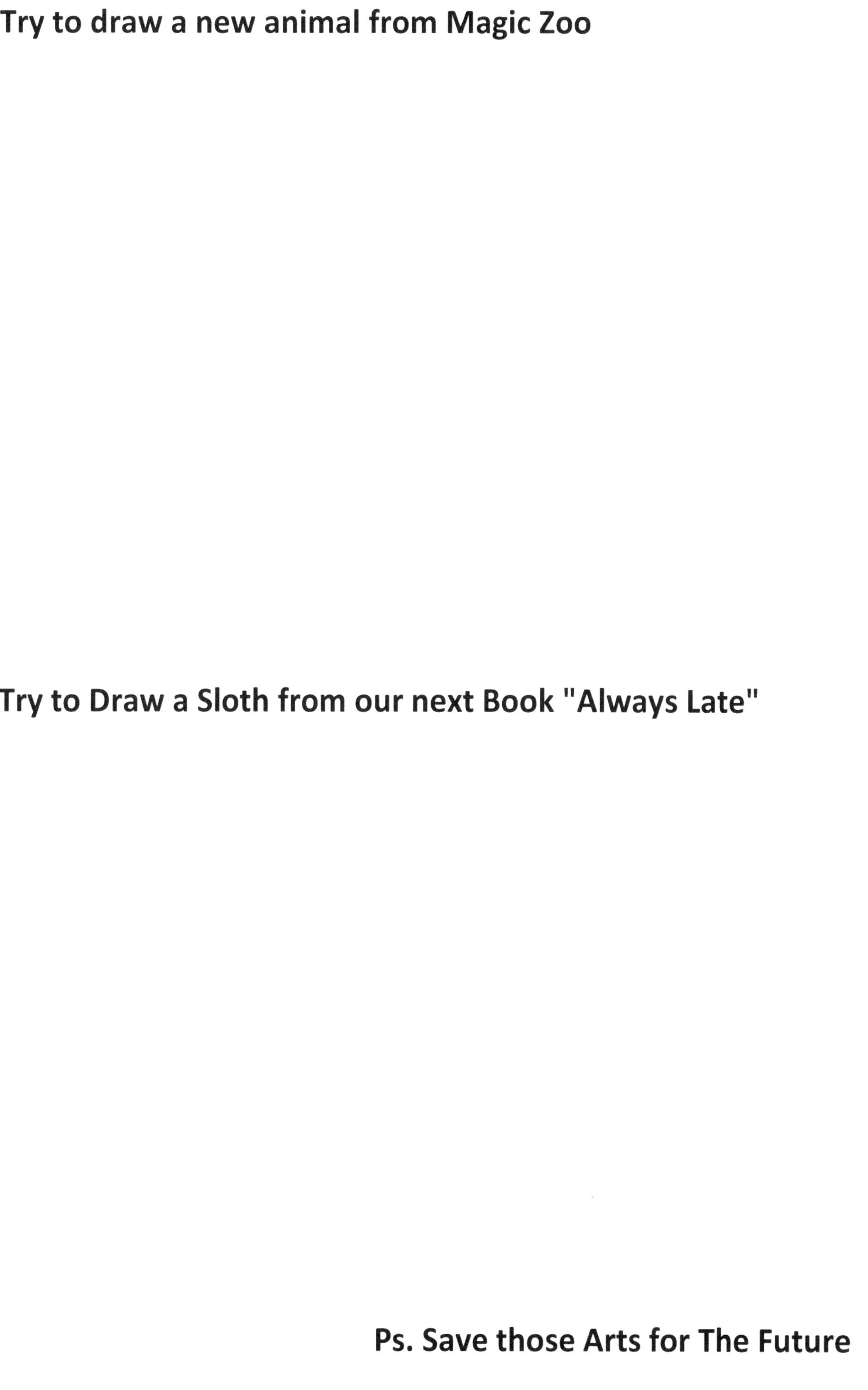

Try to Draw a Sloth from our next Book "Always Late"

Ps. Save those Arts for The Future